I AM NOT A TREE!

by Kelly Leiter

illustrated by Debbie Gillund

·HUGS-N-BEANS·
Publishing

For my son Jonathon,
who taught me that
discovering who you are
sometimes comes from
knowing who you are not.

HUGS-N-BEANS Publishing
Text copyright©2021
by Kelly Leiter
illustrations copyright©2021
by Debbie Gillund
ISBN: 978-1-7379491-0-7

The door screamed an angry sound.
Jonathon dashed into the kitchen where Mom
was making something
that smelled like home.
Crying out to his mother,
his words were
mixed with
tears.

"I hate school! I hate mean people!"

His mother bent down to wipe his wet red cheeks.

"Sometimes I hate school, too," she said.

"You don't go to school..."

"Oh, yes, I do. Everyone does. My school is called 'Life'."

"Hmmmm..." Jonathon replied, "I thought school was called Elementary."

"What Happened?" Mom asked.

"There's this kid in my class and he calls
me names, like 'Toot-head' and 'Bubble Eyes'."
He looked down and sighed. "All the other
kids laugh."

"He calls you bad names, huh? Well,
you don't have to worry about it because
we both know you are just a tree."

"WHAT??!"

Jonathon declared,

"I AM NOT A TREE!"

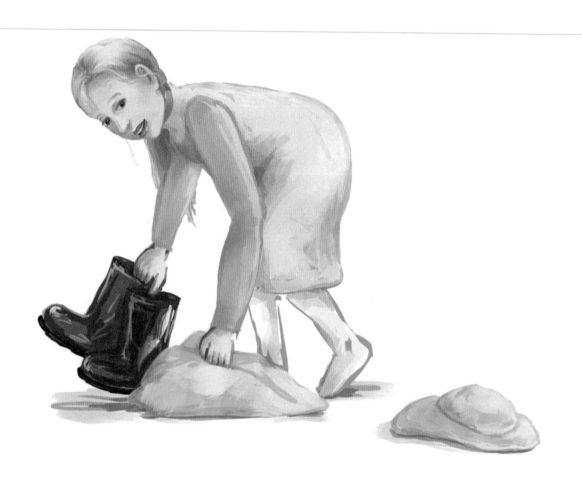

"Yes, you are, Jonathon. Now go put away

your books and get ready for supper."

Jonathon walked out of the kitchen wondering what was wrong with his mom.

Sometimes he was too loud
in the house or forgot to wash
his hands, but he was quite sure
he was NOT a tree!

That evening when Jonathon was playing with his toys, he looked up at his mom and asked, "Can I hit that mean boy tomorrow when he calls me names?"

"Absolutely not!" Mom answered.
"Remember, you don't have to worry
about that anymore because we both
know you are just a tree."

"A tree??? Trees are outside.
They have leaves and branches!! Come
here, Mom, I'll show you a tree!"

"No, that's okay," she replied.
"I don't need to do that. I am looking
at one right now."

Jonathon felt upset
as he picked up his toys.
He turned and reminded
her, "I AM NOT A TREE!"

Before bed, Jonathon was brushing
his teeth. He looked in the mirror...
He knew the face looking back
at him. There were blue eyes,
a few freckles,
and brown hair...

but no leaves or
branches.

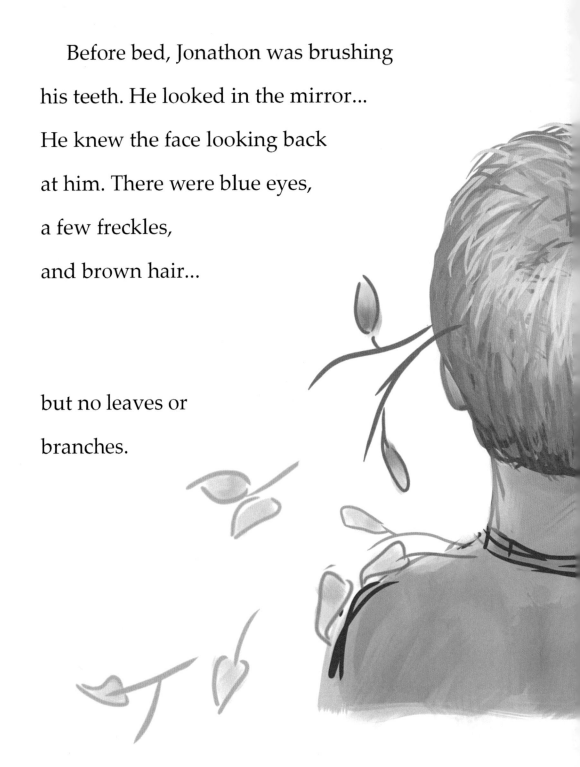

He giggled at his silly mom.

He was very sure he was just a boy!

That night his mom came to tuck him into bed. She gave him his favorite kiss on the forehead and snuggled up just like he liked.

"Why did you keep calling
me a tree today?" he asked
her in the soft night light.

"How do you know you are not one?" she replied.

"Because I know I am a boy. I have arms and legs... I like to run and play... I'm good at catching frogs and playing baseball.

"Trees look different. They are big wood plants. They have leaves, branches, and birds' nests. I climb them almost every day!"

"So did it bother you when I called

you one?" his mom asked.

"It did at first. It made me kind of mad. Then I looked into the mirror and thought it was silly so I laughed."

"Why did you laugh?"

"Because I know who I am and what I am. You were wrong. I even felt a little sorry for you. No matter how many times you say it, it won't make me a tree."

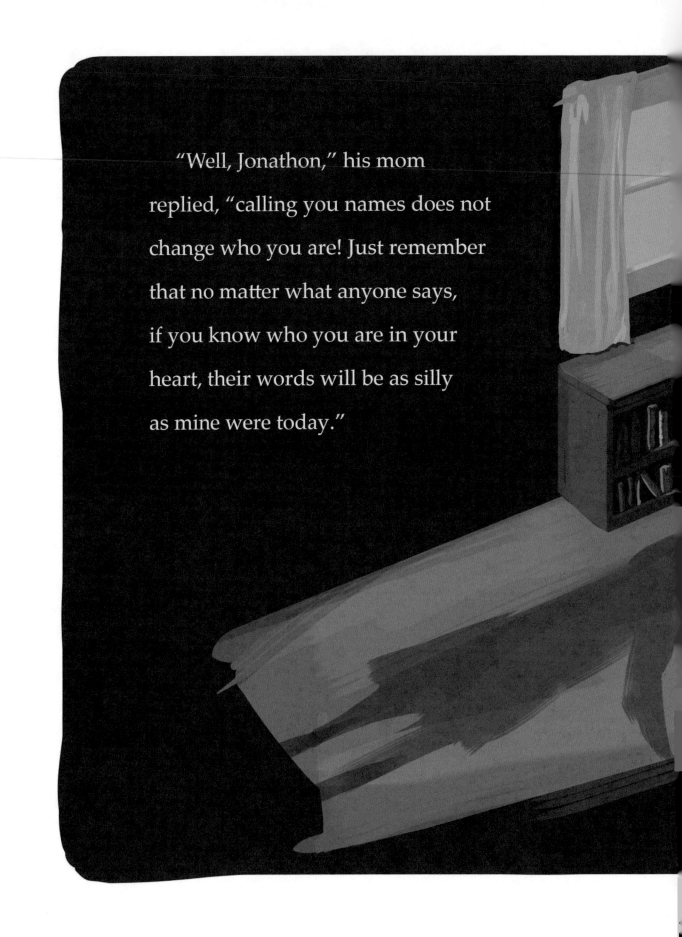

"Well, Jonathon," his mom replied, "calling you names does not change who you are! Just remember that no matter what anyone says, if you know who you are in your heart, their words will be as silly as mine were today."

Jonathon smiled as he thought

about going back to school...

The next day, the door opened with a happier sound. Jonathon's face was cheerful again.

"What happened at school today?" his mother asked.

"That silly boy called me 'dooty-breath' and said I have horse hair!" he responded.

"Oh really??? What did you do?"

"I smiled and laughed as I told him...

I AM NOT
A TREE!!!"

In memory of

Jonathon Barrett

1983 - 2000

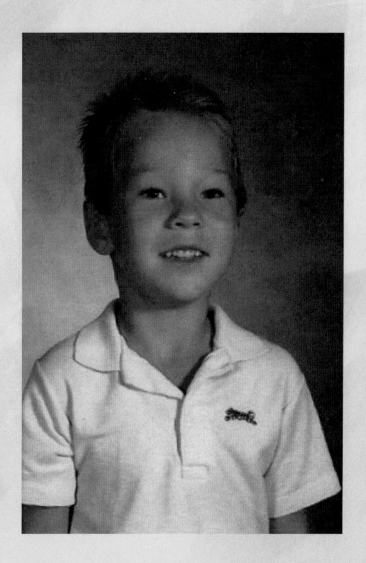

About the author:

Kelly Leiter has been an educator at heart since first grade. She recalls her mother receiving a note that read, "Please tell Kelly that I am the teacher!" She officially began her career in 1982 and is still not ready to retire. Her life's purpose is to be a true reflection of God's unconditional Love and Grace. She wrote this story based on a real-life experience with her son and has shared it in many classrooms, workshops, teen camps and seminars throughout North America.

About the illustrator:

Debbie Gillund inherited her love of art from her maternal grandmother, who painted with her at an early age and always had the foresight to put down a tarp. She has a Bachelor of Fine Arts from the University of Calgary, Canada, where she currently resides with her supportive husband, their two creative kids, and the least graceful cat known to humankind.

According to
www.stopbullying.gov

In one large study, about 49% of children in grades 4-12 reported being bullied by other students at school at least once during the past month, whereas 30.8% reported bullying others during that time.

Parents, school staff, and other caring adults have a role to play in preventing bullying.

They can:

✓Help kids understand bullying. Talk about what bullying is and how to stand up to it safely.
✓Tell kids bullying is unacceptable.
✓Make sure kids know how to get help.
✓Keep the lines of communication open.
✓Check in with kids often. Listen to them.
✓Know their friends, ask about school, and understand their concerns.
✓Encourage kids to do what they love.
✓Special activities, interests and hobbies can boost confidence, help kids make friends, and protect them from bullying behavior.
✓Model how to treat others with kindness and respect.

Made in the USA
Middletown, DE
14 February 2022